# Mega Hatch

First published by Allen & Unwin in 2018

Allen & Unwin
83 Alexander Street
Crows Nest NSW 2065
Australia
Phone: (61 2) 8425 0100
Email: info@allenandunwin.com
Web: www.allenandunwin.com

A Cataloguing-in-Publication entry is
available from the National Library of Australia
www.trove.nla.gov.au

ISBN 978 1 76029 603 2

For teaching resources, explore
www.allenandunwin.com/resources/for-teachers

Cover and text design by Sandra Nobes
Set in 16 pt ITC Stone Informal by Sandra Nobes
This book was printed in November 2017 at
McPherson's Printing Group, Australia.

1 3 5 7 9 10 8 6 4 2

macparkbooks.com

MIX
Paper from
responsible sources
FSC® C001695
www.fsc.org

The paper in this book is FSC® certified.
FSC® promotes environmentally responsible,
socially beneficial and economically viable
management of the world's forests.

# BOOK 7
# Mega Hatch

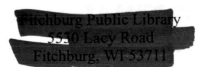

ALLEN&UNWIN
SYDNEY · MELBOURNE · AUCKLAND · LONDON

# Chapter One

Hunter, Charlie, Ethan and Ms Stegg were at D-Bot Squad base. They were staring at a big screen. Drone-cam alerts were flashing and beeping.

The alerts were for dino-eggs.
The team had brought four eggs
from an island back to base.
Now they knew there were
more eggs still out there.
Lots more eggs. And they knew
that plenty of those eggs had
already hatched. That meant
lots of new dinosaurs needing
catching.

'We have to go back to the island,' Charlie cried.

'There are eggs on those other islands too!' Ethan added.

'I'll send other D-Bot Squad teams there,' said Ms Stegg. She turned the map to live-cam. 'Now let's get a better look at what's out there.'

Hunter's eyes darted across
the screen. He pointed.

'Look! Something is moving on
that beach on the left.'

ZOOM

As the live-cam zoomed in
on the island, Charlie gasped.
'Wait! Something's moving in the
forest on top of the island too.'

'Yes, I see it,' said Ms Stegg.
'Zooming in there now.'

What they saw made their
mouths drop wide open.

'Four triceratops and six
ankylosauruses!' Hunter cried.

'Why didn't Dino Corp know about these dinos?' asked Ethan.

'They must all have hatched from eggs,' Ms Stegg said.

'Can we look at that beach now?' Hunter asked.

Ms Stegg zoomed in on the beach where he'd seen movement.

'Are they...velociraptors?' Charlie asked.

'Yes, and there are six of them!' said Hunter.

'That's sixteen dinos on the loose, Ms Stegg!' Hunter said.

'And they've grown so fast,' Charlie added. 'Just like the ones we froze in the ray-bubble.'

'This is crazy!' cried Ethan. 'We'll need the best plan ever to catch them all.'

# Chapter Two

Ms Stegg nodded slowly at the three D-Bot Squad members.

'Team, it's time to start thinking. You can do this!'

Ms Stegg handed them some snacks. 'Brain food will help. I'll go and deal with the eggs on the other islands.'

'Let's start with the raptors,' Hunter said.

Charlie nodded. 'The beach is closed in with cliffs.'

'So, we corner them and cover them with a net,' Ethan added.

Hunter smiled. 'Now for the six ankies. They're plant-eaters like the stegs. They'll be farting like crazy!'

Ethan munched on some popcorn. 'That's okay. Our helmets have gas masks.'

'Hunter found that out a bit late,' Charlie said. 'After he passed out from toxic steg farts!'

The talk of steg farts got
Hunter thinking.

'What if we had a fart-buster?' Hunter said slowly.

Ethan laughed. 'You want to bust some farts?'

'I want to suck them up and store them,' Hunter said.

'Aha!' Charlie cried. 'We could use anky farts to knock out the four tops. Then ray them. Smart thinking!'

Ethan cheered. Then he frowned. 'It will take *a lot* of farts for four tops, though,' he said.

'Let's feed the ankies lots of fart-making food, then,' Charlie said. 'We'll use a super-sized packet of massive moss. The steg who knocked Hunter out with its farts loved eating that.'

Hunter grinned. 'That's our
plan for the tops done, then.
Now, how do we catch the
ankies, once we've sucked up
their farts? There are even more
of them.'

'We'll need to steer clear of their swinging club-tails,' Ethan said. 'They'll smash us to bits.'

'And they're covered in body armour,' Charlie added.

'But not on their bellies,' said Ethan. 'Once they're on their backs, they can't turn back over—'

'And we can ray them!' cried Charlie.

'What an awesome idea, Ethan,' said Hunter. 'Now, how to flip them over...'

Hunter worked fast on a new gadget. Then he said, 'Check this out.'

'Perfect,' Charlie said. 'We need
to build our d-bots now.
Quickly! All those dinos will be
trashing the island. Every
second counts!'

'What do we need?' said Hunter.
'For the raptors, we'll need
speed, wings…'

'And to be small,' Charlie added.

'Small, fast and winged is good,' Ethan agreed. 'That should help with the ankies and tops, too.'

'And let's add mega-magnets,' Charlie added. 'Just in case we need to join together to get bigger later.'

'Good thinking,' agreed Hunter.

Charlie said, 'Let's give our d-bots club-tails, too – like the ankies. We'll need one net, for the raptors. And each d-bot will need a fart-buster and four flip-jacks.'

'Why four flip-jacks each?' asked Ethan.

'Two for each of the six ankies,' Charlie said. 'They might not be so easy to flip.'

Hunter pressed the parts button on the screen. 'Done,' he said.

Parts dropped from the machine on the wall.

'Let's build one d-bot at a time, together,' said Charlie. 'It will be quicker.'

Ms Stegg came back into the room. 'Team, I have two new gadgets for you.' She handed some boxes to Ethan.

'The long gadget is an egg-scan,'
said Ms Stegg. 'Use it to scan
the island for eggs.

'These boxes will keep any eggs
safe. Nothing will hatch inside
them. The torch on the side of
the boxes is an X-ray. It lets
you see what's inside the eggs.'

The team took the gadgets.
Then they climbed onto their
d-bots.

'Time to go,' said Charlie.

Hunter counted down: **'Three,
two, one...'**

'Good luck, team,' Ms Stegg said.

'Now!' said Hunter.

# Chapter Three

The team landed on the raptor beach. The six dinos were at the other end. They were racing in and out of the water.

'I think they're looking for food,'
Ethan said. 'They really are
trapped, aren't they? They can't
fly, and they can't climb the
cliffs. This is going to be easy.'

Hunter watched the raptors charging around. *They are just like little turkeys*, he thought. *And they're mega-fast.*

'Okay, team,' he said. 'Let's round them up!'

The team flew towards the raptors, taking them by surprise.

'Squark! **Squark!** **Squark!**'

The screeching raptors sped along the sand, like racing cars. The team had made their d-bots as fast as possible. But the dinos were faster.

'We need to work like sheep-dogs,' Charlie shouted.

The team dropped a bit lower. They pushed the raptors into a corner.

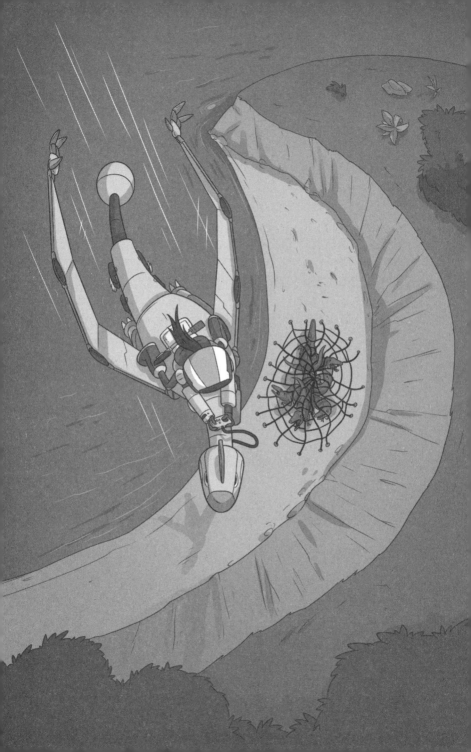

'Game on!' Ethan cried.

'Move in closer,' Hunter said. 'We want them in a tight group.'

'I'm dropping the net now,' said Charlie. The net fell over the raptors.

'Squark! **Squark!** Squark!'

'It's okay,' Hunter called to them. 'You're safe.'

'Let's do this fast,' Hunter said.
'The net won't hold them for
long.'

The team hit their d-bands'
teleport buttons. Three rays
shone down onto the raptors.
The net and the little dinosaurs
vanished.

'Done!' Ethan cheered.

# Crack! 'Screech!' Crack!

'Oh, no!' Charlie said. 'More baby raptors are hatching.'

Ethan's eyes were wide. 'There are stacks of them. And they're growing – fast.'

'We can pick them off, one by one. Only if we're quick,' said Charlie.

'Go, go, go, team dino-hunters!' Hunter shouted.

The team chased the baby dinos, raying as they went.

'Even baby raptors are born super fast,' said Ethan. 'No wonder they're called the speedy thief!'

Soon all the baby dinos were gone. The team landed on the sand.

'Do you think that's all of them?' Charlie asked.

Hunter kicked up some sand. 'Not a chance. There will be more eggs buried in this sand. I think we need to split up.'

Charlie nodded. 'Ethan and
I will scan the beach for eggs.
You see what the other dinos
are up to.'

Hunter smiled. *It's good being
with other kids like me,* he
thought.

He climbed back onto his d-bot
and flew towards the ankies
and tops.

Soon, Hunter's d-band buzzed. Charlie and Ethan had finished checking the beach. Both their egg-boxes were full.

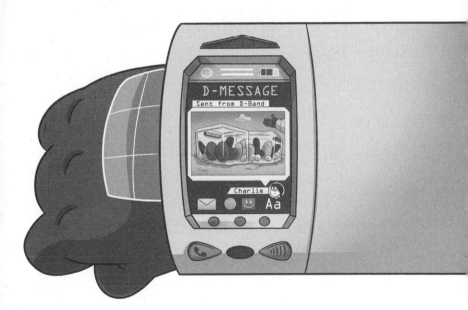

Hunter hit his d-band's talk
button. 'They're not all raptor
eggs, are they?' he asked.

'No, they're all sorts of shapes,'
Charlie said. 'I really hope
none break.'

'I'm glad the boxes keep the
eggs frozen in time,' Ethan said.

'Get on up here,' Hunter said.
'I have something to show you!'

# Chapter Four

Hunter was flying in a circle,
above the island's forest clearing.
Charlie and Ethan found him.
They flew over the trees and
joined him.

'What's happening, Hunter?'
Charlie asked.

'Take a look down there,' Hunter
said. 'Those ankylosauruses and
triceratops are getting ready to
charge!'

Charlie and Ethan looked down.

'The clearing is about to become
a dino-battle!' Ethan shouted.

'We can't let the tops and the ankies come together,' Hunter said. 'They'll hurt each other. Who has the massive moss packet?'

Ethan checked his tool belt. 'I have it. I'll lay the moss across the ankies' path. They'll eat it and fart heaps.'

'Then we can suck up the fart-gas in the fart-buster,' said Hunter. 'And use the farts to catch the tops.'

'Sounds good. But watch the ankies' club-tails, everyone,' Charlie warned. 'Flying around their bottoms is not very safe.'

'Gas masks on, everybody!' said Hunter. He hit the gas-mask button on the side of his helmet. So did Ethan and Charlie.

Ethan flew down to the ground. He added water to the massive moss packet. It grew. Ethan tipped the moss onto the ground. It grew more, into giant moss mounds.

The ankies ate the moss greedily. Their farts were very loud. Charlie and Hunter could hear them up in the sky.

# Flrrrrrpt! Braaaaapt! Phrrrrrr!

The squad members all flew to the anky bottoms. They needed to store the farts from two anky bottoms each. Their fart-busters sucked fart-gas busily.

Suddenly Charlie shouted: 'Hunter, watch out!'

# Thwack!

Hunter's d-bot spun upwards, then down towards the ground. An anky's club-tail had broken one of his wings.

'I'm out of control!' he cried. 'I can't fly any more!'

'I'm coming,' Ethan said. 'I'll use my mega-magnet to join our d-bots together.'

'Thanks, Ethan! I'll catch the last farts,' said Charlie.

Hunter was spinning very fast. It was hard for Ethan to get close.

Ethan used the mega-magnet on his d-bot. He hoped the magnet would pull Hunter's d-bot towards it.

But the magnet wasn't near enough to Hunter. Ethan flew as close as he could get. 'Come on,' he cried.

They were about to crash. But
Hunter's d-bot touched the
magnet just in time.

'Yay!' Ethan cried. 'Now to put
you down safely.'

Ethan set Hunter and his d-bot gently onto the ground.

'You saved me,' Hunter said. 'Thanks, Ethan!'

Charlie landed her d-bot next to them. 'My fart-buster is full,' she said. 'What about yours?'

Hunter and Ethan checked their fart-busters. They nodded. 'Ours are full too,' Ethan said.

'That's lucky, because the moss is all gone,' Charlie said. 'And the ankies are on the move again. Time to flip them over now!'

'My d-bot can't fly any more,' said Hunter. 'So Ethan and I have joined our d-bots. Our double d-bot flies well!'

# Chapter Five

Charlie, Ethan and Hunter
hovered above the forest
clearing. The ankies and the
tops were about to go into
battle.

Hunter watched the ankies carefully. 'Their tails are flying around like whips,' he said.

'Ready to play "Dodge the Dino"?' Ethan asked.

'Yes, I'm ready,' Charlie agreed. 'And to play "Zip and Flip"! Good luck, everyone.'

'Go, team D-Bot Squad!' Ethan cried. 'Six cranky ankies on their backs. Let's ray them, before the tops take one more step.'

Charlie ran towards her d-bot. 'I hope my d-bot can still fly.'

But one of its wings was smashed.

Ethan and Hunter landed
beside Charlie.

'There's no time to fix your d-bot
now,' said Hunter. 'We need to
join up into a triple d-bot.'

Charlie stood her d-bot up and
climbed on. Hunter pushed his
mega-magnet button.

**Snap!** The three d-bots became
one.

'We rock at dino-bot-building!'
Charlie said. 'Let's ray these
cranky ankies. Up we go!'

The triple d-bot rose above the
flipped ankies. 'Now!' Ethan
cried.

Three rays shone down onto six
dino-bellies. The ankies
vanished.

'It's amazing,' Hunter said. 'I'll
never get used to seeing that
happen!'

'It's so great knowing that they're
safe now, too,' Charlie said.

'And that we saved them!'
Ethan added.

Hunter grinned. 'Now it's time to test-drive my toxic-fart attack.'

'Let's hope we caught enough farts to knock the tops out,' said Charlie.

'I'll bet nobody's ever tried this before,' said Ethan.

'Fart-busters ready, team,' Hunter said. 'Let's give these tops all we've got.'

The squad members flew
towards the three tops.

'Okay, team,' Hunter called.
'Fart away!'

Stinky gas shot from the three fart-busters. Fart clouds covered the big heads of the dinos.

# Crash!

'One down,' Charlie said. 'I hope they don't get hurt as they fall.'

# Booom! Crash!

'Two more down,' said Charlie.

'We did it!' Ethan cried. 'All three tops on the ground.'

The triple d-bot dropped down into the cloud of farts.

'They look like they're sleeping,' Hunter said in awe. 'I can't believe we're hovering just above three real triceratops. They're awesome!'

Charlie nodded. 'Who'd believe us, even if we were allowed to talk about this? We'd better ray them now. We don't know how long they'll be still for.'

The team pushed their d-bands' teleport buttons. The three rays worked quickly.

Hunter smiled. 'And that's the tops done,' he said.

# Rumble! Shake! Rumble! Shake!

'What's that?' asked Ethan.

'Uh-oh,' said Hunter. 'There were *four* tops before. We rayed three. There's one left!'

'Do we have any fart-gas left?' Charlie asked.

'No fart-gas. No moss. No flip-jacks and no net. Just us, on our triple d-bot,' Ethan said.

'Growl! Roar! Growl!'
Rumble! Boom! 'Growl!'

'That sounds like more than just one tops,' Hunter said. 'Let's fly up and see.'

The triple d-bot rose over the trees.

'Oh!' Charlie gasped, pointing. 'Look, T-rexes! *Three* of them, rising out of that big dust cloud.'

Hunter gulped. 'We haven't planned for this,' he said. 'We'd better find our last tops before they do. T-rexes loved battling tops, and they always won.'

But when the dust settled, Hunter gasped. Trapped in the middle of a T-rex circle was their last tops. How could they save it?

Can D-Bot Squad take on
the T-rexes and win?
Read Book 8, *Dino Corp,*
to find out...